Corn
What It Is, What It Does

by Cynthia Kellogg

illustrated by Tom Huffman

Greenwillow Books New York

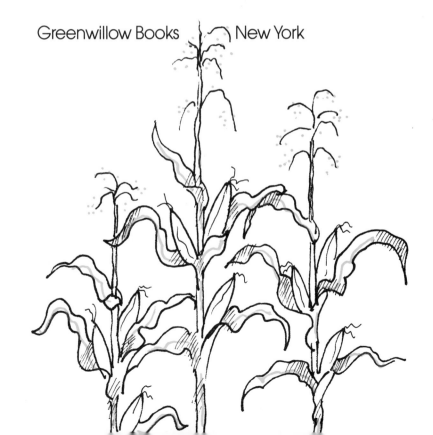

Library of Congress Cataloging-in-Publication Data

Kellogg, Cynthia.
Corn—what it is, what it does / by Cynthia Kellogg;
pictures by Tom Huffman.
(A Greenwillow read-alone book)
p. cm.
Summary: Provides an introduction to corn, where
and how it is grown, how it is eaten, and its many
uses in the home, school, and in industry.
ISBN 0-688-08024-3.   ISBN 0-688-08026-X (lib. bdg.)
1. Corn—Juvenile literature.
2. Corn—Utilization—Juvenile literature.
[1. Corn.]   I. Huffman, Tom, ill.
II. Title.   SB191.M2K195   1989
633.1′5—dc19   88-18784   CIP   AC

ACKNOWLEDGEMENTS

At the United States Department of Agriculture, Washington, D.C.:
Charles Van Lehr, Agriculture Section, Field Crops; Paul Putnam,
Agricultural Research, Central Plains Area; Kate Alfriend, News
Division.
F. Scott Riefsteck, Tolono, Illinois, corn farmer.
Edith Monroe at the Corn Refiners Association, Inc., Washington, D.C.
Philip Ingram at J.I. Case, Racine, Wisconsin, for agricultural
equipment information.
Don Coles at Martha White Foods Corporation, Brentwood,
Tennessee, for milling information.

FOR DOROTHY
AND MARY
—C. K.

JOY FOR
MICHAEL NATHAN
—T. H.

CONTENTS

INTRODUCTION

Corn Is an American Plant

Before Columbus discovered
the New World,
corn grew only
in our hemisphere.
The Indians in North,
Central, and South America
had grown it
for many centuries.

Corn has been found in places
where Indians lived more than
five thousand years ago.
The cobs are so old
they have turned to stone.
When Columbus landed
in the West Indies,
the Indians gave him corn
to take home to Spain.
From there, corn spread quickly
around the world.

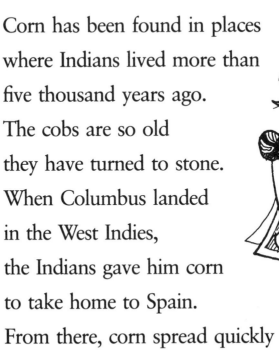

THE INDIANS
CALLED CORN
"MA-HIZ."
LATER IT
BECAME
KNOWN
AS MAIZE.

Corn and the Early Settlers

Corn helped start our country.
The earliest settlers
might have died
during their first winter
if the Indians hadn't given them
corn to cook and eat.

They showed the settlers
how to grow it.
They dug holes in the ground,
dropped in some kernels
and small fish,
then covered them.
The fish fertilized the soil
to help the corn grow.

The corn was made into

bread,

porridge,

soup,

fried corn cakes,

and pudding.

Since there were no animals
to supply milk for the babies,
mothers made a substitute
out of corn and the juices
of boiled chestnuts
and hickory nuts.

Corn was so valuable
the settlers used it
instead of money.
They traded it with the Indians
for food and furs.

As more people arrived in America,
they moved westward to find land
on which to farm and grow corn.

CHAPTER ONE

WHAT IS CORN?

The Corn Family

Corn is a grass.

Its seeds are cereal grains.

There are seven kinds of corn:

DENT, which is also called "field" corn,

is our major crop.

It is used to make food,

animal feed, and industrial products,

and for export.

FLINT is similar to dent and is used

for the same purposes.

Most of it is grown

in South America.

WAXY is raised to make
special starches
for thickening foods.

SWEET or "green" corn is eaten fresh,
canned, or frozen.

POPCORN is a favorite snack food.

INDIAN has white, red, purple,
brown, or multicolored kernels.
It is used for food in the Southwest
and for harvest time decorations.

FLOUR grows colored kernels, too.
In this country we grow small amounts
of blue flour corn to make tortillas,
chips, and baked goods.
In South America this corn
is grown in various colors
to make food and beer.

CHAPTER TWO

HOW WE USE CORN

Corn is in almost everything
you eat and touch.
When you wake in the morning,
you turn back the sheets,
pull up the window shades,
wash, and get dressed.

CORNSTARCH was used
to smooth the sheets
and in the making of the window shades.

CORN OIL is in the soap
with which you washed.
Like your sheets, your clothes
were finished with cornstarch.

Corn oil helped make the leather
of your shoes.
For breakfast your cereal may be
cornflakes.
If you ride to school in a bus
or on a bicycle,
cornstarch was used to make the tires.

There may be ETHANOL in the gasoline.
Ethanol is an alcohol made from corn.
It is mixed with gasoline to create
"gasohol" that operates cars
and other motor vehicles.
Ethanol stretches our country's
supply of gasoline.

At school,
the pages of your books
are treated with DEXTRINS.
Dextrins are roasted starch.
They form a sticky substance
that smooths the paper
and protects it from moisture.
Dextrins are also
in the printing ink
and in the book bindings.

You may eat a sandwich
of peanut butter and jelly
for lunch.
There is cornstarch and
CORN SYRUP
in the bread
and in the chocolate
in the milk.

In your gym class,
you may rest
against a wall.
There is corn oil
in the paint
and cornstarch
in the insulation.

It is your birthday
and dinner is special tonight.
There is chicken,
which was raised on corn.
There are canned peas, rice,
salad with mayonnaise,
and cake made from a mix
with canned frosting.
Everything except the rice
and salad greens
has corn in it.

The candles and matches
are made with dextrins.

After dinner
you open your presents.
One of them
is a transistor radio.
Its batteries
have cornstarch in them.

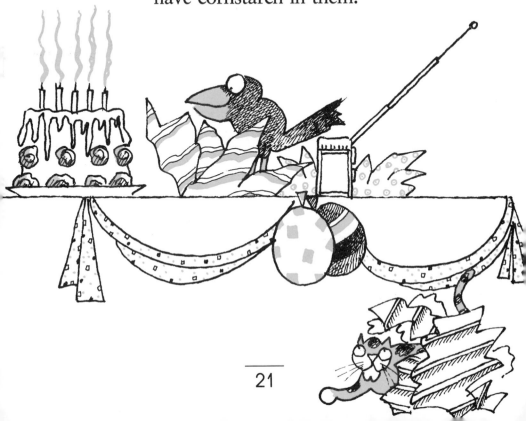

CHAPTER THREE

FARMING CORN

The
Corn
Belt

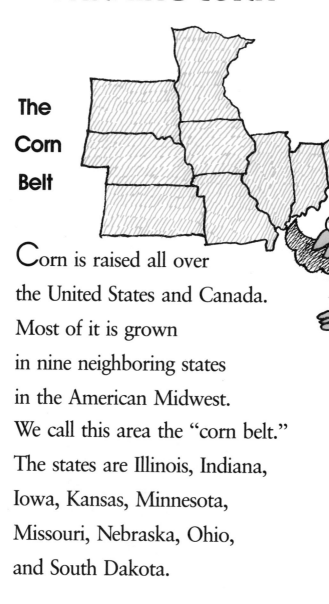

Corn is raised all over
the United States and Canada.
Most of it is grown
in nine neighboring states
in the American Midwest.
We call this area the "corn belt."
The states are Illinois, Indiana,
Iowa, Kansas, Minnesota,
Missouri, Nebraska, Ohio,
and South Dakota.

The farmer and his wife
plant the crops,
do the bookkeeping,
and work in the fields.
The children help care
for the animals,
chickens, and vegetable garden,
and they mow the lawns.

MOST CORN FARMS
ARE AT LEAST
ONE HUNDRED ACRES
IN SIZE.

The Farmer's Tools

The Tractor

The tractor pulls the machines
that cannot move on their own.
When the farmer wants to use
one of these machines
he hitches it to the tractor.

Some machines turn over
the ground.
One spreads fertilizer.
Another does the planting.
It digs the furrows,
drops in corn seed
and insecticide,
then covers the furrows.

The Combine

In fall, the combine
is brought out of its shed.
It is so huge that its tires
are as tall as a man
of average height.
It looks like a space machine,
especially when its lights
are turned on
so the farmer and crew
can work at night.
A row of giant steel points
sticks out in front.
They are called
"row dividers."

As the combine is driven
across the field,
it catches the corn stalks
between the row dividers.
The ears are snapped off
by "snapping rolls"
and dragged by chains
into the combine.
The stalks fall on the ground.

The ears enter the "rotor,"
a metal cylinder that rotates
at such a high speed
that the husks and kernels
are rubbed off the cobs.

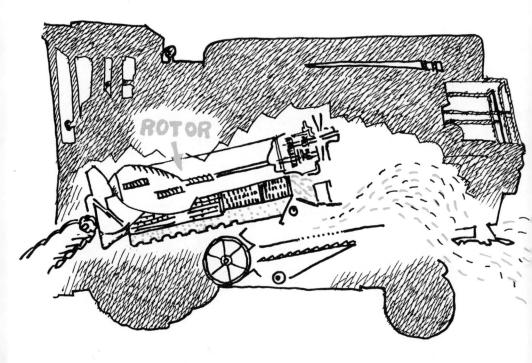

The broken-up cobs and husks
are blown onto the ground.
With the stalks
they form a blanket
that protects the soil
from erosion.
A truck takes the kernels
to the farm's storage tanks
or to a commercial storage building.
Even with a wonder machine
like the combine, the harvest
can take six or more weeks.

CHAPTER FOUR

FROM FIELD TO MARKET

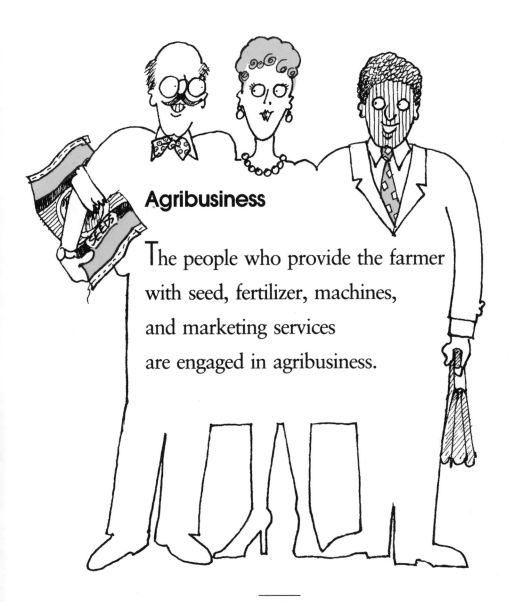

Agribusiness

The people who provide the farmer
with seed, fertilizer, machines,
and marketing services
are engaged in agribusiness.

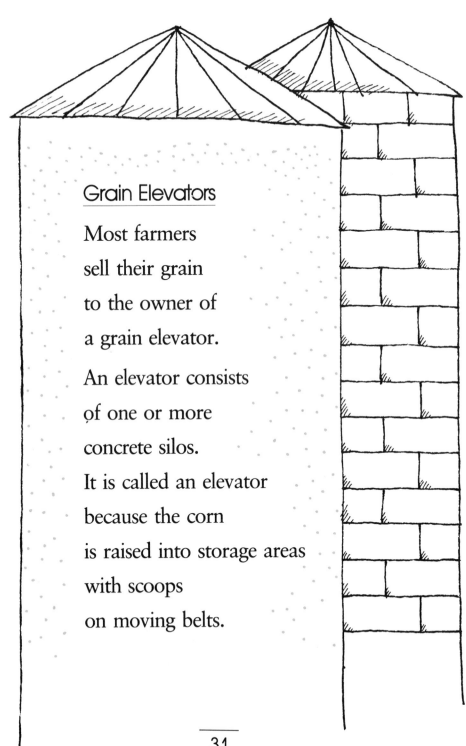

Grain Elevators

Most farmers
sell their grain
to the owner of
a grain elevator.

An elevator consists
of one or more
concrete silos.
It is called an elevator
because the corn
is raised into storage areas
with scoops
on moving belts.

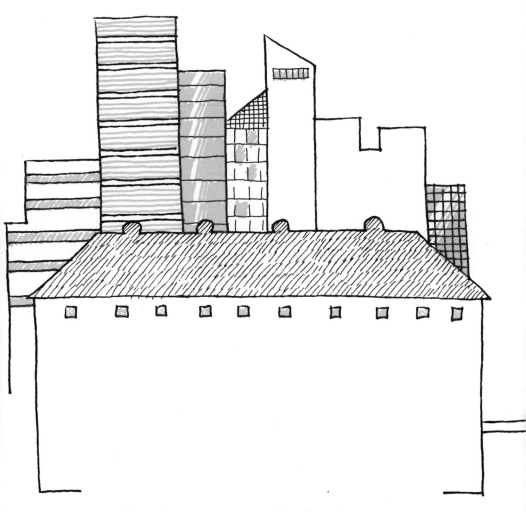

The elevator owner sells the corn
to a larger warehouse in a city
that is a major transportation center.

From there,
the corn is shipped
to mills and refineries
in our country
and is sent to countries
throughout the world.

Making Food and Other Products

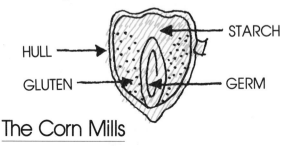

HULL

GLUTEN

STARCH

GERM

The Corn Mills

The word "mill" means to grind.
The mills grind kernels
into meal and flour for making
bread and other baked goods.
They ferment some corn
to create beverage alcohol.
They separate the germ
and the hull
from the starch.
The starch is called
the "grit."

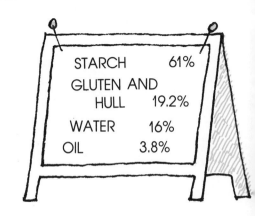

STARCH	61%
GLUTEN AND HULL	19.2%
WATER	16%
OIL	3.8%

A **CORNFLAKE**
IS A GRIT COOKED
WITH FLAVORINGS
AND VITAMINS,
PRESSED FLAT,
TOASTED, AND
SPRAYED WITH
MORE VITAMINS.

The mill sells the germs, gluten, and hulls to animal-feed companies. It sells the grits to companies that make cereal, snack foods, and beer.

SOME MILLS MAKE
HOMINY
BY TREATING GRITS
TO SOFTEN THEM.
IT IS USED FOR
BREAKFAST FOOD
AND AS
A VEGETABLE.

The Refineries

Some farmers sell their grain
directly to a refinery.
A refinery purifies a natural substance
and converts it into other products.
Petroleum and sugar cane
are examples of natural substances
that can be refined.
Corn is another.

The corn refinery is a group
of buildings connected by pipes.
The corn travels through the pipes
from building to building.
Along the way,
the kernel is separated into its parts.
The germ is removed
and processed into corn oil
and corn germ meal.

The meal, hull, and gluten
are sent to a plant
that makes animal feed.
The starch is washed and dried
to be used in food
and industrial products.

It is roasted to make dextrins.
It is converted into corn syrup,
and into high fructose
and dextrose
(glucose) syrups.

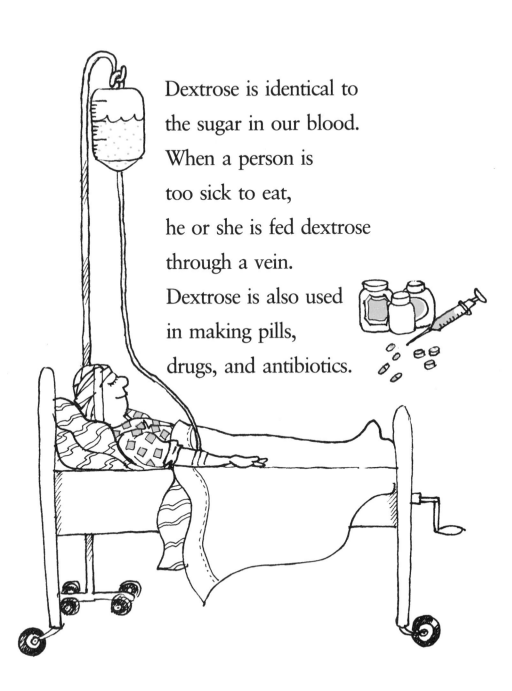

Dextrose is identical to
the sugar in our blood.
When a person is
too sick to eat,
he or she is fed dextrose
through a vein.
Dextrose is also used
in making pills,
drugs, and antibiotics.

High fructose syrup
is sweeter than sugar,
so less of it is needed
to sweeten.
It is used
to reduce calories
in many foods.

The Canners and Freezers

Corn to be canned or frozen
is grown near factories
so it can be processed
at the peak of sweetness.
Some companies
grow their own corn;
others contract with
local farmers
to raise it.

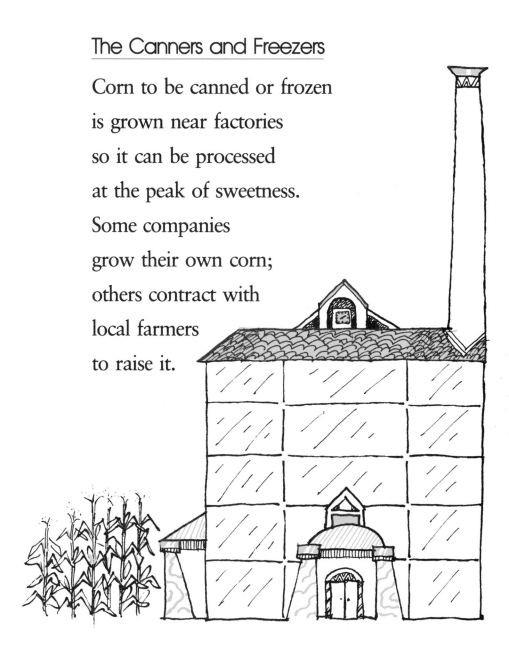

CHAPTER FIVE

THE SUPERMARKET

The supermarket sells
about 1,300 foods
that contain corn.
High fructose syrup
is used to sweeten
soft drinks, frozen desserts,
canned fruit, jam, jelly,
and many other foods.
It is also used in
some diet foods.
Dextrose works with yeast
to make bread rise.
It is also used
to ferment light beer.

Cornstarch is used
to thicken desserts,
pie fillings, soup, and yogurt.
It is added to snack foods
before they are fried,
so they will absorb
less oil.

Corn syrup helps
to prevent crystals
from forming in ice cream.
It helps canned fruits
and vegetables
hold their shape.

CONCLUSION

You don't have to see a corn field
or walk into a supermarket
to be reminded of corn.
Day or night,
you can just reach out
to touch one of the many
thousands of things
necessary to our lives
that corn is a part of.
Corn is as precious to us
as our gold and silver,
our coal and water,
our forests and oil.

HOW WE USE THE CORN WE GROW

(Figures based on a typical year's crop.)

Source:
U.S. Department of Agriculture

DENT/FIELD

THE MAJOR CROP:
8,877 MILLION BUSHELS,
ALMOST HALF
THE WORLD'S OUTPUT

FLINT

WAXY

POPCORN

SWEET/GREEN

INDIAN

FLOUR

	AMOUNT	
	In millions of bushels	Percent of crop
Animal Feed	4,095	50%
Storage, minor uses	2,366	22%
Exports to other countries	1,241	14%
High fructose syrup	339	4%
Alcohol (mostly ethanol plus alcoholic beverages and industrial alcohol)	335	4%
Dextrose/Glucose	185	2%
Ground corn (grits, meal, hominy, etc.)	161	2%
Starch	155	2%
Oil	(Extracted from corn used for all the products above)	
Similar to dent; grown mostly in South America	UNKNOWN	
Starches	TOO FEW TO COUNT	
Snack food	10	
Canning, freezing, eating fresh	275	
Eaten in Southwest; used for harvest decorations because of its many colors	TOO FEW TO COUNT	
Grows in many colors; used for many purposes in South America. Blue corn is grown in United States for chips, tortillas, and bread.	TOO FEW TO COUNT	

After her graduation from Radcliffe College, CYNTHIA KELLOGG went to New York, where she worked as a reporter and editor for *The New York Times,* as a writer and editor for the *Ladies Home Journal* and *Woman's Day,* and as managing editor of *Venture,* a travel magazine. She writes about gardening, collectibles, decorating, travel, and subjects of interest to women.

TOM HUFFMAN attended the School of Visual Arts in New York City and holds a B.A. from the University of Kentucky. Mr. Huffman is a free-lance artist whose works have appeared in galleries, advertisements, and national magazines. He has illustrated many children's books, including nine Greenwillow Read-alone Books.